Now, who thought they'd ever he[ard] [ ]'t fly? It's like saying that some fish [ ] ns can't roar. Well, we know that t[ ] roar because there is a story written about one, and it's a really interesting story!

This little story is about a little baby bird known as a Bald Eagle. Her name was Softy. Softy's Dad's name was Baldie, and her Mom's name was Swoopie.

Baldie and Swoopie had their own nest which was about two feet deep.

Even though Softy only weighed a pound when she hatched from her egg, she would grow much, much bigger and this is why their nest needed to be so big.

Once Softy was able to speak, she had lots of questions. One day she asked her Dad, "Why does everyone call you Baldie? You have feathers."

Baldie replied, "Because when I was born, my head was bald. Even though we eventually grow feathers, we are still known as *Bald* Eagles."

"And how did I get my name?" Softy asked curiously.

"Your head was also bald when you were born," said Baldie. "Before the few feathers you have now started to grow, your whole body was bald and pink and so very soft. That's why we called you Softy."

Softy then turned to her Mom and said, "How about you, Mommy... how did you get the name Swoopie?"

"I got the name Swoopie because I *swoop* down toward the water, very fast, to catch fish."

"But *how* do you catch them, Mommy?" said Softy.

Swoopie showed Softy her hands.
"Our hands are called talons.
See how long our talons are?
They're the reason we catch fish so easily!
Our talons are *so* strong that we can carry fish that are very big *and* very heavy."

A few days later, because Softy's talons were so big, she started to crawl up the side of her nest. Baldie and Swoopie were just getting ready to fly out when they looked over and saw little Softy fall out of the nest.

What a *terrible* thing!
Baldie and Swoopie weren't too worried because they expected that Softy could fly at this young age.

But *no...* even though Softy was flapping her tiny wings really fast... she couldn't fly.

Well now, before little Softy could hit the ground, Swoopie *swooped* down and caught her, saving her from being seriously hurt.

Both Baldie and Swoopie were worried about their baby girl now. Why couldn't she fly?

So, they decided to teach her to fly. They put her back into the nest and said, "*Jump...* jump and flap your wings."

Softy jumped, but sadly she *still* couldn't fly. Again and again she tried, but *nothing* worked. *'What to do?'* wondered Baldie and Swoopie. Then they decided to send their little Softy to the neighborhood *Flying School*.

"Let's go," said Swoopie to Softy. "Jump on my back and we'll fly to flying school."
"Will you come with us, Daddy?"
Softy asked. "I'm a little afraid to fly on Mommy's back."
"Don't be afraid," said Baldie, "I'll fly next to you. I wouldn't miss your first day at flying school for anything."

So, off they flew with Softy sitting happily on Swoopie's back.

They were so happy
about school that they
began to sing.

*"Off we fly to school today,
to school today, to school today...
Off we fly to school today,
on such a wonderful day."*

As the family landed they were
greeted by the owner of the
Bird Flying School,
Mr. Jolly Hooter.
Mr. Hooter was an owl.
He wore glasses and a funny
hat; at least, that's what
little Softy thought it was.

But Baldie and Swoopie knew
that Mr. Hooter's hat was really a flying helmet.
Mr. Hooter placed a smaller funny hat on Softy's
little head. "This is your helmet," he said,
"and you'll also need a parachute."
"A what?" said Softy.

"A parachute! You'll need this if one of your wings doesn't flap the way it should. If you think there's a problem, you should pull on this cord.

The parachute will open and you'll gently glide to the ground. Do you understand?" asked Mr. Hooter.

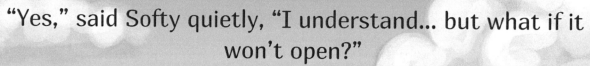

"Yes," said Softy quietly, "I understand... but what if it won't open?"

"Don't worry," said Baldie. "I'll be with you. If the parachute doesn't open, I'll be there to catch you!"

"Ready to go?" said Mr. Hooter. "You can even sing a song as you glide. If you find you can't fly, the ride in the parachute will still be fun, and your Mom and Dad will be alongside you the whole way...

...Good luck!" he said giving little Softy a thumbs-up.
"Thank you, Mr. Hooter," said Softy, and up went her little
thumb as she flew away on Swoopie's back.
Sure enough, Softy started to sing again.
"Not to worry, I won't hurry...
I'm going to have some fun today!"
Her voice was beautiful, and she kept laughing as she
sang. Up in the air they flew as a family.

When they were flying much higher than the nearest tree, Swoopie looked back at Softy. "Are you ready?" she asked.

Softy made sure she had the parachute cord
safely in her talons. "Okay!" she said. "I'm ready."
"*Okay!*" said Swoopie.
"*Jump,* Softy. Everything will be fine!"
Softy jumped and tried to quickly flap her wings, but she
just kept falling. "Oh, my!" she said, "*I can't fly.*
I hope my parachute opens."

Yes, indeed! Softy pulled hard on her parachute cord and just like Mr. Hooter said, the small little parachute opened right over her head. As it opened, Softy was bounced back into the air just like a rubber band. *WOW,* that was quite a jerk!

Softy looked around and, sure enough, there was Baldie flying alongside her. "I'm right here," said Baldie. "Good job opening that parachute!"

"But I can't fly..." Softy cried, "...what am I going to do?" But then Swoopie's eyes widened and she said, "I have an idea! You can sing better than any other bird. We'll enter you in the *Golden Bird Talent Contest.*
If you win, you can give concerts for all the animals and birds... around the world.

You can fly around on my back, and Daddy will fly along with us."

The *Golden Bird Talent Contest* is held once a year, and *every* bird who has *any* unusual talent enters the contest.

Softy agreed to enter that year's Golden Bird Talent Contest which was just two weeks away.

The next morning, Swoopie flew Softy to a huge Pine tree. "Okay," said Swoopie once she'd landed, "this is the best place for you to practice your singing. I'll fly down to the ground and listen from there. The song you've chosen is *Singing In The Air.* Start singing and keep repeating the song... until you feel you can sing it anytime, anywhere."

"Okay," said Softy, "here I go...
*I'm singing in the air, just singing in the air...
what a wonderful feeling, I'm singing in the air...*"

As Softy finished the song Swoopie clapped and cheered, making a lot of noise in the trees.

Other birds who were flying around stopped to perch on nearby branches. They listened to Softy's singing, too, and when she finished they also clapped in approval and appreciation.
It was certainly the *right* song for the big show!

Well, the big day finally arrived.
The *Golden Bird Talent Contest* was about to begin.

There were about one-hundred different animals and birds,
sitting on the branches of the trees surrounding
a giant tree that looked like a big stage.
On this stage, the competing birds would
perform their acts.

From up in the sky, Charlie the Red Robin from France flew
down and landed on the stage.
He'd won the previous year's *Golden Bird Award,*
by performing triple summersaults in the air.

Charlie introduced Blinky, the Master of Ceremonies
for the show. Down flew Blinky the beautiful white Parrot
from Brazil, dressed in a smart black tuxedo with a bow tie.

He was well-known for
telling funny animal
stories, and was also
a past winner of the
Golden Bird Award.

In minutes
the show began.

Blinky first introduced Sharpie the Woodpecker
from Canada who could make the funniest sounds
while pecking away at a piece of wood.
Sharpie got a big applause from the audience.
Then Blinky introduced Harpy the happy Hummingbird
from the Caribbean who was able to hum fifty
different songs, one after the other.

She hummed five of her favorite
songs for the audience and when
she hummed *Singing In The Air,*
the same song that Softy
was going to sing, Softy loved it.

It was now Softy's turn to be introduced.
Blinky told the audience that Softy was a Bald Eagle
who *couldn't* fly...
but she'd overcome her problem flying
by learning to sing beautifully.

"So, ladies
and gentlemen..."
said Blinky,
"...let's give little Softy
a *big* welcome!"
The animals waved
and clapped loudly
as Swoopie flew Softy
down to the big-tree stage.

Softy was wearing a cute red and blue hat with a white star. After all, she was a Bald Eagle, the national bird of the US. There was some chatter when Softy started to sing. Then suddenly the audience became quiet. Softy began to sing her song and smiled as she did. It certainly seemed as though the audience liked what they were hearing.

After all the other birds had performed their acts, Blinky told everyone that the judges would decide *who* was going to be the winner.

Perky the Giant Stork from Japan chose Softy as the winner. Slinky the Pigeon from England chose Sharpie the Woodpecker. Perky and Slinky then looked at Josie the beautiful Swan from Malaysia, and waited for her vote. She paused, looked up at the sky and said,

"I vote for... Softy!"

That was it! Two out of three votes meant that the winner of the *Golden Bird Award* was Softy the Bald Eagle.

"Let's bring Softy out on the stage and give her the award."

Softy hopped over to the center of the stage. Blinky stood there with the award; a large, beautifully carved and polished wooden wing mounted on a flat piece of wood.

Every year, the Woodpecker family was responsible for crafting the Golden Bird Award.

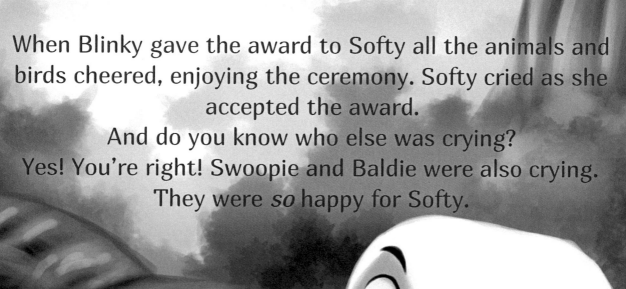

When Blinky gave the award to Softy all the animals and birds cheered, enjoying the ceremony. Softy cried as she accepted the award.

And do you know who else was crying?

Yes! You're right! Swoopie and Baldie were also crying.

They were *so* happy for Softy.

Softy had proven that anyone *can* overcome their disability, by finding just *one* thing that they *can* do. And it's that one thing that will make their life enjoyable and worth living!

We end our little story now, by telling you that not only did little Softy become an award winning singer; soon afterwards, she began to sing for disadvantaged and elderly birds and animals at different hospitals in the forest.

Before she knew it she was travelling around the world, using her new found talent to bring joy and happiness to everyone she could!

Fun Facts
For You

Bald Eagles usually live for between twenty and thirty years.

Some Bald Eagles' nests are as deep as six to ten feet.

Most other birds' nests are not nearly as deep. Most birds usually weigh less than half a pound at birth, but baby Bald Eagles can weigh as much as a pound when they are born, and can grow to weigh as much as twenty pounds. Female Bald Eagles are usually four or five pounds heavier than male Bald Eagles are.

Bald Eagles lose their grey down feathers at the age of six-weeks-old. By the time they are ten to thirteen-weeks-old, their black juvenile feathers will have grown.

You can see the Bald Eagle symbol on all American paper dollars.

The Bald Eagle is famous in America because it is the American national bird. It's also the national animal of the United States of America and appears on the seal of the US.

Bald Eagles can be found in many states of Northern America, especially in Alaska. They are also found in Canada.

Bald Eagles are usually found around large lakes and alongside rivers and streams. This is because their most important food is fish.

All Eagles' talons are made of Keratin, the same thing that our hair and nails are made from.

Young Bald Eagles will attempt to fly for the first time at the age of three-months-old.

Bald Eagles can fly down to the water's surface to catch a fish at ninety miles an hour. Their normal flying speed is thirty miles an hour, which is also very fast.

Bald Eagles are closely related to African Fish Eagles which are found in the continent of Africa.

When Woodpeckers peck away at a piece of wood they make as many as twenty pecks per second.

In most cases boy birds are brightly colored, and girl birds have brown earthy colorings. But with Red Robins, both have bright red chests and it can be difficult to tell the difference between them.

Not only can some Parrots mimic human words, some actually understand the words they speak. They can recognize objects and learn the sounds of the words for the objects. They don't have vocal cords like we do; instead they whistle from their throats.

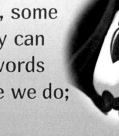

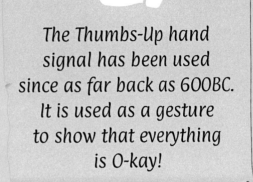

The Thumbs-Up hand signal has been used since as far back as 600BC. It is used as a gesture to show that everything is O-kay!

Hummingbirds are the only birds that can fly forwards, backwards, sideways and upside down, and they can flap their wings 200 times per second.

In the olden days, Pigeons were trained to carry messages from one person or place to another. They can fly as far as 500 miles in one day.

Your voice has the power to create harmonies and melodies through singing. When we hear harmonious and melodious singing, also from birds, a hormone called Serotonin is released in our body. This hormone is known as 'the feel-good hormone', and it is known to heal most illnesses.

Of the nineteen species of Storks around the world, seven of them live in Malaysia. The Saddle-Billed Stork from Africa stands as tall as five feet and has a wingspan of nine feet.

White Swans usually only ever have one partner in life. If one partner dies, the other won't find a new one. They are loved because they move gracefully and their white feathers are associated with purity.

Acknowledgements

THOUGHTS AND THANK YOUs FROM THE AUTHOR

George Green, a former broadcasting executive, first created these stories then told them to his children more than fifty years ago.

Recently his delightful, funny and interesting animal stories became a reality, thanks to many members of his family - especially his son, Randy Green, who assembled an outstanding creative team to assist George in writing and publishing his books.

Each member of the team comes from a different part of the world, and thanks to technology they were able to communicate as though they all live in the same neighborhood.

A special thank you to Carly van Heerden (South Africa) who is an amazing editor, and also an author with a few books to her name. Her contributions cannot be overstated.

Our talented Indonesian-based illustrator, Nidhom (iNDOS Studio), made the characters *jump* off the pages in George's books. The word *creative* cannot begin to describe how good an artist he is.

Also, a thank you goes to Dianti Andajani, also from Indonesia, who helped with communication.

Thank you also to Xenia Janicijevic-Jovic from Serbia, our book designer who did a great job with the form, structure and content placement for the stories.

Bottom line... George is blessed with a great publishing team!

Thanks to all!

Softy, the bird who couldn't fly

By George Green

First Printing, 2014

Made in the USA
San Bernardino, CA
10 October 2015